Dear Parents:

Congratulations! Your child is taking the first steps on an exciting journey. The destination? Independent reading!

STEP INTO READING® will help your child get there. The program offers five steps to reading success. Each step includes fun stories and colorful art or photographs. In addition to original fiction and books with favorite characters, there are Step into Reading Non-Fiction Readers, Phonics Readers and Boxed Sets, Sticker Readers, and Comic Readers—a complete literacy program with something to interest every child.

Learning to Read, Step by Step!

Ready to Read   Preschool–Kindergarten
• big type and easy words • rhyme and rhythm • picture clues
For children who know the alphabet and are eager to begin reading.

Reading with Help   Preschool–Grade 1
• basic vocabulary • short sentences • simple stories
For children who recognize familiar words and sound out new words with help.

Reading on Your Own   Grades 1–3
• engaging characters • easy-to-follow plots • popular topics
For children who are ready to read on their own.

Reading Paragraphs   Grades 2–3
• challenging vocabulary • short paragraphs • exciting stories
For newly independent readers who read simple sentences with confidence.

Ready for Chapters   Grades 2–4
• chapters • longer paragraphs • full-color art
For children who want to take the plunge into chapter books but still like colorful pictures.

STEP INTO READING® is designed to give every child a successful reading experience. The grade levels are only guides; children will progress through the steps at their own speed, developing confidence in their reading.

Remember, a lifetime love of reading starts with a single step!

Copyright © 2020 Disney Enterprises, Inc. and Pixar. All rights reserved. Published in the United States by Random House Children's Books, a division of Penguin Random House LLC, 1745 Broadway, New York, NY 10019, and in Canada by Penguin Random House Canada Limited, Toronto, in conjunction with Disney Enterprises, Inc.

Step into Reading, Random House, and the Random House colophon are registered trademarks of Penguin Random House LLC.

Visit us on the Web!
StepIntoReading.com
rhcbooks.com

Educators and librarians, for a variety of teaching tools, visit us at RHTeachersLibrarians.com

ISBN 978-0-7364-4099-8 (trade)
ISBN 978-0-7364-8294-3 (lib. bdg.)
ISBN 978-0-7364-4100-1 (ebook)

Printed in the United States of America   10 9 8 7 6 5 4 3 2 1

Disney · PIXAR

SOUL

Journey to You

adapted by Natasha Bouchard

illustrated by the Disney Storybook Art Team

Random House 🏠 New York

Joe Gardner
is a music teacher.
He loves music.
Most of all,
he loves
playing jazz.
Jazz inspires Joe.

But teaching music
is not Joe's dream.
He wants to be
a famous jazz musician.
Joe finally gets his chance!

He auditions for
a well-known jazz band.
Joe impresses them
with his piano playing.
He will be in their show.

Joe is very excited.

He is also very distracted.

All of a sudden,

he falls down a manhole.

Joe is now a glowing soul.

He is on a walkway

moving toward The Great Beyond.

Joe panics!

He pushes past the other souls

and leaps off the walkway.

Joe lands in a beautiful place.

It is where new souls

get Earth Passes.

Once they have a pass,

they can go to Earth.

Joe wants an Earth Pass, too.

Then he can play in the show.

Joe pretends to help a new soul.

He is matched with

a stubborn soul named 22.

But 22 does not want

to go to Earth at all.

22 says she will

give Joe her Earth Pass.

He can go to Earth

in her place.

But first they must find

22's special Spark.

Joe says this Spark is her purpose.

They go to the Hall of Everything.

22 tries a lot of different jobs.

She is a baker, a firefighter,

and even an astronaut.

22 does not like any of them.

They are not her Spark.

22 has a different plan.

They will need

Moonwind's help.

Moonwind helps lost souls.

Moonwind can help Joe

return to Earth.

He opens a portal,

and Joe sees his own body.

He is in the hospital!

A cat is curled up on his legs.

Impatient, Joe jumps into

the portal and bumps

22 in with him.

Joe is in the hospital,
but something is wrong.
Joe is in the cat's body,
and 22 is in Joe's body!

They flee the hospital.
They must find a way
to get Joe back
into his own body.

They escape into the city.

22 is overwhelmed

by the city streets.

Joe brings 22 pizza.

The pizza makes her feel better.

She wants more.

But they are running out of time.

Joe's jazz show is in a few hours.

They find Moonwind on Earth.

He will help them.

They will meet again

before Joe's show.

At Joe's apartment,

22 helps Joe's student.

Then 22 starts to wonder

about life on Earth.

For the first time,

22 wants to see

more of Earth.

22 lives Joe's life for a day.

She tries new things.

She meets new people.

22 thinks Joe has

a wonderful life.

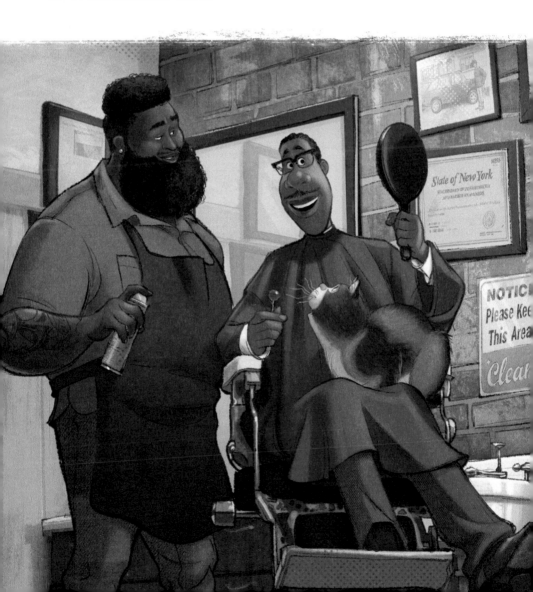

Joe cannot wait

to get back into his body.

But 22 has second thoughts.

She wants to stay on Earth.

Joe tells her she is not ready.

22 still doesn't know her Spark.

Meanwhile, someone
from the Soul World
has realized that Joe is missing.
She tracks him down on Earth.
She captures Joe and 22.

Joe and 22 are back

in the Soul World.

22 finally gets her Earth Pass,

but she gives it to Joe.

22 does not believe

she has earned it.

Joe goes back
to his life on Earth.

Joe finally plays with
the famous jazz band.
He lives his dream.
He feels happy—
but not for long.
After the show,
he feels disappointed.
He thought his life
would change.

Joe plays the piano

and thinks about 22.

Joe was so busy

chasing his dream,

he forgot what was important.

He wants to make things right.

Joe returns to the Soul World.

22 has become a lost soul.

She missed her chance

to live her own life on Earth.

Joe now knows that

22 is ready for Earth.

He wants to tell 22.

But no one can catch her.

Joe finally stops 22

and returns her Earth Pass.

He tells 22 she is ready.

Joe says that 22's love for life
is her Spark.
She already knows
what is important in life.
Joe helps 22 go to Earth.

Suddenly, a special
Earth Portal appears.
Joe is given another chance!
He will go back to his life.
Joe can't wait to see what's next.